Butterfly Wishes

Blue Rain's Adventure

The Butterfly Wishes series

The Wishing Wings
Tiger Streak's Tale
Blue Rain's Adventure
Spring Shine Sparkles

Butterfly Wishes

Blue Rain's Adventure

Jennifer Castle
illustrated by Tracy Bishop

BLOOMSBURY
NEW YORK · LONDON · OXFORD · NEW DELHI · SYDNEY

First published in the United States of America in April 2018
by Bloomsbury Children's Books
www.bloomsbury.com

Bloomsbury is a registered trademark of Bloomsbury Publishing Plc

For information about permission to reproduce selections from this book, write to
Permissions, Bloomsbury Children's Books, 1385 Broadway, New York, New York 10018
Bloomsbury books may be purchased for business or promotional use. For information on
bulk purchases please contact Macmillan Corporate and Premium Sales Department at
specialmarkets@macmillan.com

Library of Congress Cataloging-in-Publication Data
Names: Castle, Jennifer, author.
Title: Blue Rain's adventure / by Jennifer Castle.
Description: New York : Bloomsbury, 2018. | Series: Butterfly wishes ; 3
Summary: The Wishing Wings call on sisters Addie and Clara to help a
newly emerged, very grumpy butterfly, Blue Rain, while they also
help a mischievous neighbor, Oliver.
Identifiers: LCCN 2017021642 (print) | LCCN 2017037381 (e-book)
ISBN 978-1-68119-375-5 (paperback) • ISBN 978-1-68119-691-6 (hardcover)
ISBN 978-1-68119-376-2 (e-book)
Subjects: | CYAC: Butterflies—Fiction. | Mood (Psychology)—Fiction. |
Friendship—Fiction. | Wishes—Fiction. | Magic—Fiction. | Sisters—Fiction.
Classification: LCC PZ7.C268732 Blu 2018 (print) | LCC PZ7.C268732 (e-book)
DDC [Fic]—dc23
LC record available at https://lccn.loc.gov/2017021642

Typeset by Westchester Publishing Services
Printed and bound in the U.S.A. by Berryville Graphics Inc., Berryville, Virginia
2 4 6 8 10 9 7 5 3 1 (paperback)
2 4 6 8 10 9 7 5 3 1 (hardcover)

All papers used by Bloomsbury Publishing, Inc., are natural, recyclable products
made from wood grown in well-managed forests. The manufacturing processes
conform to the environmental regulations of the country of origin.

For Erica Chase-Salerno,
butterfly spirit extraordinaire

Butterfly Wishes
Blue Rain's Adventure

PROLOGUE

Deep in a wooded grove, there was a jagged rock covered in bright green moss that glistened with morning dew.

A butterfly perched at the very top of the rock. She was staring up at a huge willow tree nearby, nervously fluttering her orange, yellow, and black tiger-striped wings. This was no ordinary butterfly;

this was a Wishing Wing butterfly . . . and she was magic.

"Come on, Tiger Streak!" called another Wishing Wing named Sky Dance, as she flew in circles around the tree trunk. Sky Dance's wings were brilliant pink and turquoise, with cloud patterns on them.

Tiger Streak took a deep breath and shot into the air, following her friend toward the big willow tree. They both landed on the edge of a small hollow in the tree's trunk. Tiger Streak peered into the hollow.

Inside, she saw four gray shapes hanging. Two were the shriveled remains of chrysalides that had once held caterpillars as they transformed into Wishing Wings.

"That was my chrysalis, right?" Tiger Streak asked Sky Dance, pointing to one of these with her antennae. "I remember spinning it."

"Yes," replied Sky Dance, and then she nodded toward the second opened chrysalis. "And that was Shimmer Leaf's."

Now Tiger Streak examined the other two shapes: chrysalides that hadn't

opened yet. New Wishing Wings would pop out any day now . . . or would they?

"These chrysalides should be glowing and gold," said Tiger Streak, "but they look colorless and sad."

"They're under the dark enchantment," Sky Dance explained. "Just like with you and Shimmer Leaf, when they emerge they may not know they have to grant a wish to a human child before sunset in order to earn their magic."

Tiger Streak shook her head sadly. "I still shudder to think how close I came to losing my magic forever and weakening the magic of all Wishing Wings. We have to find out who's behind this!"

"We will," said Sky Dance. "At least, I hope we will. But first we have to see if the next butterfly needs help earning her magic."

"I would say we're about to find out," said Tiger Streak. She pointed an antenna at a chrysalis that was wiggling and jiggling so much, it looked like it was dancing.

As the chrysalis slowly began to open, Sky Dance leaned in close to Tiger Streak and whispered, "Get ready!"

Both butterflies stretched out their wings, strong and straight, prepared for whatever was about to happen next.

CHAPTER ONE

Addie Gibson crouched behind an old woodpile, hugging her knees tight. She tried to breathe as quietly as she could, even though her heart was pounding. Hopefully this hiding place would keep her safe.

Then she heard a voice echo against the trees.

"Twenty-nine, thirty!" yelled Addie's

friend Morgan. "Ready or not, here I come!"

This was a seriously intense round of hide-and-seek.

Addie listened to Morgan's footsteps as they grew fainter, which meant she was walking toward the other side of Addie's backyard. *Phew*, thought Addie. Maybe Morgan would find Addie's sister Clara first.

Addie and Clara had just moved from the city to this house in Brook Forest. They'd known Morgan, their next-door neighbor, for only a day. Addie wanted to show her new friend that even though she wasn't used to playing this game outdoors, she could totally do it. She could ignore the slimy, damp ground underneath her and pretend not to see the spiderweb on the woodpile three inches from her face.

Addie hated spiders. They were so creepy. Whenever one had appeared in her old apartment, she'd screamed for help. If one popped up now, she'd probably do the same.

Then Addie remembered something.

You used to hate bees too, she told herself. *Now you know better.*

It was true. Yesterday they had met a bee named Kirby who was about as nice as anyone she'd ever met, human or insect.

Yes, she'd met a bee. Talked to him. Wasps and caterpillars too. And, of course, BUTTERFLIES! Unique, beautiful, smart, kind, brave butterflies! *Magic* butterflies.

Addie listened to Morgan sneak around the yard. Her footsteps were getting louder and closer, for sure.

It had been two short days since Addie

and Clara discovered Wishing Wing Grove, a secret place deep in the woods behind their new house. The Grove was the home of the enchanted Wishing Wing butterflies, who could do many wonderful things. Like talk, for instance. And grant wishes by turning one thing into another. The sisters had teamed up with two Wishing Wing sisters, Sky Dance and Shimmer Leaf, to help some freshly hatched butterflies known as New Blooms who'd been cursed with a dark enchantment. So far, each New Bloom had needed Addie and Clara's help to break the enchantment and earn its magic by making a wish come true for a human child . . . all before sunset on the day it emerged.

Addie could see the top of Morgan's head as she drew nearer. She prepared herself to be found. Suddenly, there was the sound of an upstairs window opening and Addie's mom's voice.

"Addie, honey! There's someone ringing the doorbell, but I'm on an important call right now. Can you go answer it?"

Addie sighed. Way to ruin a great hiding place! When she popped up from behind the woodpile, she startled Morgan.

"Ahhh!" exclaimed Morgan. "You were right there and I had no idea!"

"See if you can find Clara," said Addie with a smile. Then she sighed. "I have to get the door."

Addie hated answering the door. She never knew who would be there or what she was supposed to say to the person. But she'd done a lot of brave things in the last two days, so maybe it was time to get

over this particular fear. She walked into the house and took a deep breath as she grabbed the handle and pulled, ready to greet a stranger with a big smile on her face.

But nobody was there.

The front porch was empty. Addie stepped out and looked left, then right. Nothing.

She closed the door and turned to find Clara and Morgan standing in the hall behind her. "Who was it?" asked Clara.

Addie opened her mouth to reply. *Ding-dong!* The doorbell rang again.

Clara frowned. "Did you answer it the first time?"

"Yes!"

Now Clara sighed. "Obviously you didn't. I'll get it, because *I'm* not weird that way."

Clara flung open the door.

Nobody was there. Again.

"What . . ." murmured Clara, scanning the porch and steps for any sign of a human being.

Clara was about to close the door when they heard it: a sudden rustling of leaves.

"I know what's going on," whispered Morgan, who had stepped up behind them. "Follow me."

Morgan tiptoed down the porch steps into Addie's front yard, Addie and Clara following behind her. Then Morgan stopped, looked around, and zeroed in on a large bush near the edge of the driveway. She turned to Addie and Clara, pointing to the bush and rolling her eyes.

As Morgan crept toward the bush one silent step at a time, Addie thought,

Whoa, she's good at seeking. Next time I'll find an even better hiding place.

Morgan reached the bush, stuck her arms into it, and pulled apart the branches to reveal . . .

A face.

Which belonged to a very surprised dark-haired boy.

"Got you!" shouted Morgan.

The boy tumbled out of the bush and took off running down the driveway. His blue-and-yellow-striped shirt was a blur as he raced out of sight.

"Who on earth was that?" asked Clara.

Morgan sighed. "That," she said slowly, "was Oliver."

"Does he live on our street?" asked Addie.

"He lives right there," Morgan replied, pointing to the house next door. "We used to be good friends, actually. He used to be *nice*. Now all he does is go around pranking people. We're lucky he didn't have his squirt gun today. He loves sneaking up on kids with that thing!"

"He'd better not ever try to sneak up on me," said Clara.

"I'm sorry you guys aren't friends anymore," Addie said to Morgan.

"I'm sorry too," said Morgan. "It all started when Oliver's big brother James joined the Navy and got stationed overseas. They're super-close and he's basically

Oliver's hero. After he left, Oliver didn't talk to anyone for weeks. Then the pranking started."

Addie thought about what it might feel like for Clara to live so far away. Would she miss her? Probably not at first. She'd celebrate! Nobody to fight with. Nobody to borrow her stuff without asking . . .

"Addie!" Clara burst out, and for a moment Addie worried that Clara could tell what she'd been thinking. But Clara's face was serious, not angry, as she stepped up to whisper in Addie's ear. "I'm getting a thought message from Shimmer Leaf! They need us to come quickly to Wishing Wing Grove!"

Because Shimmer Leaf was Clara's Wishing Wing, they could send thought messages to each other. Sky Dance and Addie were connected the same way.

Addie nodded and closed her eyes, waiting for a message to come from Sky Dance. But there was only silence. That was strange . . .

"It's getting late," said Morgan. "I should get going. I promised my mom I'd help her weed the garden today."

Addie suspected that Tiger Streak, another Wishing Wing, had worked her magic to make Morgan run home. Now Addie and Clara could rush to Wishing Wing Grove without having to explain themselves. Less than twenty-four hours ago, Morgan had helped save Tiger Streak's magic, but afterward, the butterflies had used an enchantment to make Morgan forget it had all happened. Addie felt sad for her new friend, but also knew it was necessary to keep too many humans from discovering Wishing Wing

Grove. Only Addie and Clara were allowed to remember it. Still, Tiger Streak was now officially Morgan's Wishing Wing. Even though Morgan didn't know it, Tiger Streak would always be there, keeping Morgan's butterfly spirit strong.

They said goodbye to Morgan as she headed back home.

"Are you ready?" Addie asked Clara.

"Are you kidding?" Clara replied. "I'm *always* ready."

Addie took her sister's hand. Together they raced toward the line of trees that marked the edge of their backyard—and the beginning of a new adventure.

CHAPTER TWO

Addie and Clara didn't know their way around their neighborhood or town yet, but they knew exactly how to get through the woods to the magical grove. Addie smiled to think about how, just a few days ago, she was afraid to even set foot past her yard.

Eventually, the woods opened up onto a clearing. It was filled with tall green grass that waved in the wind and reminded Addie of an ocean. They had reached Silk Meadow, the entrance to the realm of the Wishing Wings. As they began walking through it, Addie looked at Clara, wondering if her sister felt as excited and nervous as she did.

When the girls were halfway across the meadow, something appeared in the air up ahead. It flew straight for them, growing bigger as it drew nearer. Addie recognized the dancing movement of fluttering wings. Then she spotted the wings' colors: purple, peach, and mint green with leaf patterns. It was Shimmer Leaf! Addie scanned the meadow for Sky Dance, knowing she must not be far behind.

"Wow!" said Shimmer Leaf when

she reached them in the middle of the meadow. "That was fast!"

"We came as soon as I got your message," said Clara.

"Where's Sky Dance?" asked Addie, still searching for her friend.

Shimmer Leaf suddenly looked very sad. She dropped quickly onto Clara's shoulder, her wings folded tight against her body.

"We don't quite know where Sky Dance is," said Shimmer Leaf softly.

Addie felt a *flip-flop* in her stomach. "Is she lost?" she asked.

"Kidnapped?" blurted out Clara. Addie gave her a dirty look. Leave it to Clara to think the worst.

"Nothing like that," said Shimmer Leaf, and Addie sighed with relief. "She's hiding somewhere and none of us can find her. But Addie, maybe you can."

Addie frowned. It wasn't like Sky Dance to hide. Sky Dance was confident and strong, fearless and positive. Something very bad must have happened.

They continued toward the cluster of trees at the gateway to Wishing Wing Grove. Shimmer Leaf took off from Clara's shoulder and landed on a nearby branch.

"Okay," said the butterfly. "So this is what we know so far. This morning at the Changing Tree, another chrysalis opened. Her name's Blue Rain. When we were caterpillars, Blue Rain was always the quiet one. Very sweet and sensitive. But when she came out of her chrysalis this morning, she was definitely not quiet. Or sweet. OR sensitive!"

"Uh-oh," said Clara.

"Uh-oh is right," agreed Shimmer Leaf. "The first thing she did was fly to a branch of the Changing Tree and start shouting mean things to everyone she saw. She called one Wishing Wing a 'six-legged freak.'"

"But all butterflies have six legs!" exclaimed Addie. "Including her!"

"Exactly," said Shimmer Leaf. "She was just being grumpy and nasty for no reason. It didn't make sense, until we realized the dark enchantment must be making her act like this."

The dark enchantment seemed to work in different ways on each New Bloom. When Shimmer Leaf had emerged from her chrysalis, the enchantment had kept her from knowing who or what she was. It had made Tiger Streak think she was a bee. *Now,* thought Addie, *it must be causing Blue Rain to rain unhappiness on everyone.*

Shimmer Leaf continued filling them in. "When Sky Dance heard, she went straight to the Changing Tree to get a handle on the situation. We know she spoke to Blue Rain. Next thing anyone saw, Sky Dance was flying straight and fast out of there. One butterfly heard her crying. Nobody's seen her since."

Addie's heart crumpled to think of Sky Dance so upset. "Blue Rain must have said something that really shook her up."

"Yes, I think so too," said Shimmer Leaf. "You have to find her, Addie. And of course, we have to help Blue Rain earn her magic and break the enchantment. But first things first."

Addie nodded, then closed her eyes. She pictured Sky Dance in her head, her magic butterfly friend's beautiful pink-and-turquoise wings covered in cloud patterns.

Sky Dance! I'm here in Wishing Wing Grove to help you. Where are you?

Addie remained quiet, her eyes shut tight. She could hear crickets in the distance. The squawk of a bird high up in a tree somewhere. The *flit-flut* of butterfly wings and the soft jingle of rushing water in the nearby creek. But nothing from Sky Dance. Addie wasn't sure this was going to work. She'd never had a magical thought connection with any-thing before. Was it like a telephone? Was there a way to "call" her friend?

Suddenly, her head filled not with a sound but . . . a feeling. A feeling of deep, dark sadness. It was so powerful, Addie let out a sob.

"What's wrong?" asked Clara, putting her hand on her sister's shoulder.

"She's hurting," said Addie.

"Who hurt her?" growled Shimmer Leaf. "Where is she hurting? Her wing? Her legs?"

"It's not pain in her body," said Addie, shaking her head. "It's pain in her heart."

Shimmer Leaf's antennae and wings drooped. "You mean . . . her *feelings* are hurt?"

"Yes." Addie was sure of it now.

"It must have been something Blue Rain said to her," said Clara.

Shimmer Leaf rolled her big bead-like eyes. "You've got to be kidding me. She flew away and hid because of that?"

"I can find her," said Addie, but inside she was thinking, *I think I can find her. I hope I can find her.* She closed her eyes again and listened. Now she heard something:

I am not, I am not, I am not, I am not.

Addie took a few steps, and the voice grew the tiniest bit louder in her head.

Am not! She's wrong! The thoughts from Sky Dance continued, and Addie let them guide her farther into Wishing Wing Grove. She moved past the Changing Tree, which was a huge willow with branches reaching and twisting in every direction. Then along the creek, its water clear as glass, its banks dotted with yellow crickets who shared the Grove with the butterflies and made catchy music. Sky Dance's thoughts stopped being words and changed to soft cries. Addie's feet seemed to know where they were going even if she didn't.

Eventually, Addie reached a willow tree on the edge of the creek. Its roots were thick and knotted, and underneath this tangle, there was a little cave of dirt and rocks. Addie sat on the biggest root and put her head between her legs so it hung upside down, looking into the blackness of the cave. She couldn't see anything, but Sky Dance's cries were louder than ever.

"Sky Dance? Are you in there?"

All was quiet for a moment. Then Addie heard a shaky voice say, "Yes."

"Will you come out and talk to me?"

After another pause, Sky Dance said softly, "Okay."

The butterfly slowly emerged from the dark. Addie put her hand out and Sky Dance climbed onto it. Addie sat upright again, a little dizzy as the blood rushed out of her head, and held her friend carefully on her palm.

"Hi," said Addie.

"Hi," said Sky Dance. "I guess you found my secret place."

"I won't tell anyone about it," said Addie. "Why were you crying? Why did you run away?"

Sky Dance took a deep breath. "There's a New Bloom named Blue Rain . . ."

"Shimmer told us. She came out of her chrysalis and started acting not-so-nice."

"She was awful!" exclaimed Sky Dance with a little sob. "I flew over to welcome her, and do you know what she said?"

"Something mean?"

"She said, 'You think you can tell people what to do because your mother's the queen!' She told me I'm not royal, I'm just a bossy know-it-all! And that she's going to call me Princess Pig-Head from now on!" Sky Dance's wings went limp and flopped to the ground. "I am not bossy! I am not a know-it-all! Sometimes I hate being a princess!"

Addie wished she could reach out and hug Sky Dance, but she knew butterfly-hugging was not really possible. Instead, she reached out one finger and gently stroked one of Sky Dance's silky, cloud-patterned wings.

"Some people are really good at finding the one thing you feel insecure about," said Addie. "In my world, we call those people bullies."

"How do you deal with them?"

"We try to ignore them. A bully wants to see you run away and cry, so if you don't do that, you've taken away that person's power over you. If we're going to break this dark enchantment, we're going to have to ignore Blue Rain too."

"Ignore her," repeated Sky Dance. "Okay. I think I can do that."

Then they heard a voice shouting, "A HUMAN?" Startled, Addie looked up to see where it was coming from. Another

Wishing Wing perched on the trunk of the tree. The butterfly's wings were bright, brilliant purple and deep blue, covered in raindrop patterns. Addie had never before thought of rain as so lovely, but in this moment, she understood that it was.

"Hi," said Addie.

"Ew, it *talked* to me," said Blue Rain with a sneer in her voice. She sounded so much like the meanest girl at Addie's old school, it was eerie. "I hate everything about humans," said Blue Rain. "But you know what I hate most?"

Addie almost replied *What?* but caught herself.

"I hate their foreheads! Why do you have foreheads, anyway? They're huge and pointless!"

Addie opened her mouth to reply, but she was so shocked, nothing came out. She'd never told anyone, but she'd always felt self-conscious about her forehead. She thought maybe it was too wide for her face.

Blue Rain laughed loud and long into the silence, then flew off.

CHAPTER THREE

Addie stared at the space where Blue Rain had been, feeling like she'd just been stung. She'd had this feeling before, whenever another kid said something mean to her and she didn't know how to respond. But she'd never expected to get this feeling from a butterfly!

"I know," said Sky Dance, flying to land on Addie's shoulder. "She's so mean."

"It's obviously the dark enchantment making her act this way, but still . . . that really hurt."

Sky Dance tilted her head sideways, thinking a bit. "This enchantment will be a tough one to break. But break it we must!" The Wishing Wing's eyes suddenly grew wide. "That's not being bossy, is it?"

"No," said Addie, laughing. "That's just being determined. Let's find our butterfly sisters and figure out how to help Blue Rain."

Suddenly, Addie heard Clara calling for her.

"We're over here!" Addie shouted back, drawing aside the hanging branches of the willow tree to see her sister and Shimmer Leaf.

"Sky!" exclaimed Shimmer, and the

butterfly sisters rushed together, flitting in joyful circles around each other. *I guess that's how you hug when you have wings instead of arms*, thought Addie.

"I'm okay," said Sky Dance. "Blue Rain was aiming to hurt me, and she did at first. But now I'm not going to let her."

"Good," said Clara. "We need to get her to the human world so someone can catch and release her and break the spell."

"That won't be easy," said Addie. "Blue Rain says she hates humans."

"Mama will know what to do," said Shimmer Leaf.

They all agreed that finding the butterflies' mother, Queen Rose Glow, was a good first step. Sky Dance led the way toward the giant boulder where the Queen, along with her husband King Flit Flash, would be holding court.

As they came upon a small hill covered with pebbles, a high voice greeted them.

"Well, hello!" chirped the voice.

Surprised, Addie turned to see a long, thin, neon-green caterpillar perched on the largest pebble. It was Queen Rose Glow's friend Madame Furia. Despite her slightly creepy appearance—she had red spikes all the way down her back—she always seemed wise and cheerful.

"Hi, Madame Furia," said Sky Dance, hovering above the caterpillar.

"What are you girls up to?" asked Madame Furia, one red eye pointing at Addie, the other pointing at Clara.

"We're on our way to talk to Mama," said Shimmer Leaf. "Blue Rain emerged this morning. The dark enchantment has made her—"

"A rather unpleasant Wishing Wing?"

Furia cut in. "I know. She came by this way and said some absolutely dreadful things about my spikes. I like my spikes! They're good for hanging things on!"

Furia smiled and winked one of her red eyes at them. Addie was about to say *Nice to see you, but we're in a rush*, when Furia took a deep sigh and kept talking.

"Of course, I hated them at first," said Furia. "They started growing right after your grandmother Queen Silver Star cast the enchantment that would keep me from becoming a butterfly."

Addie knew that Madame Furia had once been like every other caterpillar in Wishing Wing Grove—one who would, at the right time, spin a chrysalis at the

Changing Tree and emerge as a New Bloom, ready to grant a wish from a human child and earn her Wishing Wing magic. But Furia had broken the rules of the caterpillar nursery and was given a punishment: she would stay a caterpillar forever.

"I think your spikes are cool," said Clara. "Anyway, we'd love to stay and talk, but we really must be going . . ."

"Did you know my name used to be Golden Burst?" asked Madame Furia, as if she hadn't heard Clara.

Sky Dance and Shimmer Leaf landed on pebbles next to Furia. Addie saw their antennae straighten up and curl in curiosity toward the caterpillar.

"That's pretty!" said Sky Dance. "Why are you called Madame Furia now?"

"Well," said Furia, "since I couldn't

change into a butterfly, I wanted to change *somehow*. So I changed my name! I had trouble managing my temper back then . . . and the name "Furia" felt like it fit me. After all, it was my temper that got me into trouble in the first place."

"Addie," whispered Clara, tugging on Addie's shirt. "We don't have time for this."

"Yeah, but aren't you curious?" Addie whispered back. "Plus, she seems really lonely and needs someone to talk to."

Clearly Sky Dance and Shimmer Leaf were eager to listen to Furia's side of a story they'd heard their whole lives. "Mama said you two were best friends," said Sky Dance to Furia.

"We were," replied Furia with a smile. "Inseparable, in fact! But your mother was always very friendly and started spending time with another caterpillar too. I got jealous. I thought this caterpillar was trying to steal your mother away from me, and I'd be left with no friends. But instead of talking to Rose Glow about it, I did the wrong thing."

"Mama said you stole food from the nursery and made it look like the other caterpillar did it."

"Shimmer, hush!" scolded Sky Dance. "Don't be disrespectful."

"It's okay," said Furia. "She's right. That's exactly what I did. I was young, and it was a mistake. I'm happy with who I am now, although I wasn't at first. I was so angry about the punishment, I left Wishing Wing Grove."

"Where did you go?" asked Clara. Now she was sucked in too.

"Oh, I visited Wasp Point, Bee Hollow,

Ant Mountain . . . It was fascinating to see what life was like in other kingdoms!"

"Wow!" said Sky Dance. "Someday you'll have to tell us more."

"Someday?" asked Madame Furia. "Why not now?"

"We have to figure out a way to bring Blue Rain to the human world so we can help her grant a wish."

"Oh, right!" laughed Furia. "I forgot you were in a hurry. I'm so sorry. Thank you for keeping a lonely caterpillar company for a little while."

"Anytime," said Sky Dance, flying ahead to lead the way for Addie, Clara, and Shimmer Leaf. "We'll come by again soon to hear more!"

As they left Madame Furia's hill, Addie looked back to see the caterpillar smiling at them. It was nice that they'd stopped to talk to her.

After a few minutes, the two pairs of sisters came upon the large boulder where Queen Rose Glow held court. The boulder looked like the inside of a kaleidoscope, covered with the dazzling, moving colors and patterns of dozens of Wishing Wings.

Sky Dance and Shimmer Leaf flew on ahead, landing at the top of the boulder between their parents. As Addie and Clara approached, Addie heard many Wishing Wing voices talking over one another.

"She called me Shrimpy Wings!" sniffled one. "I can't help it that my wings are on the small side!"

"She said I don't know how to fly

straight," shouted another. "I fly crooked on purpose! It's more fun that way!"

Addie and Clara found a spot near the boulder and stood by quietly to watch what happened next.

"She doesn't act the way a Wishing Wing should act!" said one butterfly. "I say, let her lose her magic, and then banish her!"

There were cheers of "Yes!" and "Good idea!" coming from the other butterflies, until a loud clapping sound shook the air around them. Then another. Queen Rose Glow was banging her wings together. The red rose patterns on them lit up and sparkled in the sunlight. That got everyone's attention.

"Enough!" commanded Rose Glow. "Don't you remember? Every time a New Bloom fails to earn its magic, it weakens the magic of all Wishing Wings! I believe this is the ultimate goal of the dark enchantment. Thankfully, with the help of our human friends Addie and Clara, we have thwarted the enchantment twice. We will do it again for Blue Rain."

A murmur rose up among the gathered butterflies.

"I know it's hard," continued Rose Glow, "but you must remember, Blue Rain's behavior is not her fault. It is not the real Blue Rain acting this way. It's the enchantment. We will stand together and help her, because she's as much a Wishing Wing as every one of us."

"The Queen is right!" called Sky Dance.

King Flit Flash turned to Addie and Clara. "Do you agree, dear friends?"

Addie thought for a moment. What

Queen Rose Glow said made sense. She stepped forward.

"Yes!" said Addie. "Clara and I will do whatever we can to help Blue Rain grant her first wish."

"But how?" asked the butterfly who Blue Rain had called "Shrimpy Wings."

Queen Rose Glow's words echoed in Addie's head. *It is not the real Blue Rain acting this way.*

Then, Morgan's words from earlier: *It all started when Oliver's big brother left for the Navy.*

It suddenly became crystal clear to Addie. Oliver was also under a type of dark enchantment—an enchantment otherwise known as "sadness."

"Clara!" she exclaimed. "We've got to get Blue Rain together with that boy Oliver! He's the perfect person to catch her!"

Clara wrinkled up her nose. "Ew. Really?"

"Absolutely!" said Addie. Then she addressed the butterflies. "Clara and I have a plan. Can we count on all of you to help if we need it?"

Another murmur rose up among the butterflies.

"I will help!" shouted Sky Dance.

"Me too! Whatever you need!" added Shimmer Leaf.

"You shall have anything you need from me," chimed in Queen Rose Glow.

"And me, of course," said King Flit Flash.

Then Addie heard other butterflies piping up—"Yes!" "Me too!" "I'm in!"—and knew that once again, the Wishing Wings were united, as they should be.

"Excellent!" said Addie. "So now we need to rush home and talk to Oliver."

"Let us make your trip shorter," said Rose Glow, and she broke into a mischievous, magical smile.

Addie knew what that meant, and her heart jumped with excitement.

CHAPTER FOUR

Rose Glow and Flit Flash winked at each other. Sky Dance and Shimmer Leaf both laughed.

The Wishing Wing royal family was about to make some very special magic.

Addie took a few steps away from Clara. Then she stood very still as Rose Glow and Sky Dance zipped into the air together, touching their wings. They began to fly a circle around Addie, trailing a sparkling rainbow of their colors behind them. Red, green, silver, turquoise, pink, white. Addie closed her eyes and for the first time could *feel* the magic dancing around her. It almost tickled.

She peeped with one eye to glimpse Flit Flash and Shimmer Leaf. They were flying around Clara in the same way, their wings touching. Addie knew each

butterfly pair would fly around them three times. She wondered if she'd know when they were done.

And she did. In one amazing moment, she felt light and free. She could feel the breeze on her arms. No. Not arms. WINGS!

Addie opened her eyes and saw that she was small now, butterfly-size. Her wings always came out of the magic

looking the same: magenta and powder blue, with lavender hearts on them. *This must be what my butterfly spirit looks like,* she thought.

Clara laughed. She also had the same wings as before: deep pink and orange, with flames on them.

"No time to admire yourselves!" said Rose Glow. "Hurry home!"

Addie knew the magic would wear off in a few minutes. If they flew quickly, they could make it.

"Come on!" she shouted, turning to Clara. But Clara had already taken wing, so then Addie had to yell, "Wait for me!" and rocket herself into the air.

"They're no slowpokes!" laughed Shimmer Leaf as she whooshed off behind them. Sky Dance followed.

The two pairs of sisters flew out of

Wishing Wing Grove and over the dancing grass of Silk Meadow. Into the woods, past trees that Addie recognized even though they were much bigger now. Or rather, she was much smaller. She looked down and saw her own footprints from before. How strange that she didn't have those feet at the moment! She felt light and fast and fearless.

In no time at all, the butterflies were zooming past the trees behind Addie's house. Whoa! Their backyard looked huge from here! And their house looked like a mansion. One a giant might live in. Addie giggled at how weird and wonderful it all was.

"Hey," said Clara, flying close to Addie. "Let's keep going. We can take a tour of the neighborhood while we're up here!"

"Definitely!" shouted Addie. Now she

took the lead; she wasn't going to let Clara be in charge the whole time. They sped past their house—it looked even bigger from the front!—and toward the road. They followed the road in a direction they'd never been, past one, two, then three houses. Addie saw an elderly neighbor walking two huge dogs, a baby playing in a kiddie pool with his mother nearby, and a chalk drawing of a monster on a driveway.

"We should probably head back to your yard," warned Sky Dance, flying close to her. "Make sure you land where no humans can see you."

Addie nodded. She circled around the third house and into that backyard, over the head of a man mowing his lawn. In the next backyard, a woman was sitting in a chair, working on her computer.

This is like spying, said Addie to herself.

When she reached the next backyard, Addie saw sparkles flashing in her eyes. She felt herself flying slower, and her body seemed heavier. She knew the magic was wearing off and headed for the ground, hoping she could pull off a soft landing. Fortunately, there was nobody in this yard.

A gentle *thud,* and then suddenly she was rolling in grass.

"Ow!" she heard Clara shout.

"Clara, you're going to have to work on recognizing when it's time to land!" said Shimmer Leaf. She and Sky Dance had come to rest on a nearby rock. "Are you okay?"

"I will be in a minute," replied Clara as she took a deep breath. "Where are we?"

"One of the neighbors' backyards, I guess," said Addie, sitting up and wiping grass off her face. She looked around and saw their own house through some trees. "Oh! We're right next door to home!"

"Right next door?" repeated Clara slowly.

"Yup!"

"But that means . . . this must be Oliver's house." Clara's voice was full of dread.

"Holy moly, you're right," said Addie. "It'll be super awkward if he sees us here. Let's go around and knock on the front door."

"I'll catch up in a minute," said Sky Dance. "When we were flying, I got some pollen on myself and it's driving me crazy." She began cleaning her left antenna with her two front legs.

Addie and Clara crouched low, as if they were pretending to be cats, and ran as quickly and quietly as they could toward the side of the house. Shimmer Leaf fluttered along next to them.

"Not. So. Fast."

The girls froze and slowly turned around.

Oliver was standing before them, his hands on his hips. It was like he'd dropped out of the sky (and she'd thought they were the only ones who could do that!). Addie glanced up and saw a treehouse above their heads. Okay, so maybe he *had* dropped out of the sky . . . sort of.

Addie gulped, then cleared her throat.

She wasn't good at meeting new people, especially in weird situations like this.

"Hi!" said Clara extra-cheerfully before Addie could open her mouth. Clara was much better under pressure. "You must be Oliver!"

"And you must be the new girls," he said, not sounding the least bit friendly or excited about it.

"Yes, we live—"

"Right next door," said Oliver, rolling his eyes. "Duh. I know. What I don't know is, why are you in *my* backyard?"

Addie finally found her voice. "We were just . . ." she began, not sure how to finish the statement.

"You're here to prank me, aren't you? To get even for that thing with the doorbell."

"No, we're not!" said Addie.

"Give me a break. Of course you are. I'm sure Morgan told you all about me."

"She did!" said Clara, stepping toward Oliver and standing just like him, with her hands on her hips. She looked confident and brave. "She told us you used to be nice, and that the two of you were friends. And now you go around pranking everyone and have no friends anymore. We can see why! We just came over here to say hi, and look how you're treating us!"

Oliver looked at them, his lip trembling.

Addie felt glad Clara had stood up to him, but also a little sad for him, too.

"Shut up!" exclaimed Oliver. "Go away!" He sniffled, then ran around the corner of his house.

They all paused for a few moments, not sure what to do next. Addie hoped Oliver would change his mind and come back.

"Come on," said Clara finally, tugging on Addie's sleeve. "Let's go home and brainstorm."

Shimmer Leaf landed on Clara's shoulder and said, "You're right. He does need a wish. The trick will be getting him to catch Blue Rain. Are you coming, Sky Dance?"

But Sky Dance didn't answer.

Addie looked over to the rock where

Sky Dance had been just a few seconds ago, but the butterfly was gone.

There was only Oliver standing next to it.

With a butterfly net.

And Sky Dance trapped inside.

CHAPTER FIVE

N o!" squealed Shimmer Leaf.

"Let her go!" shouted Addie.

Clara didn't say anything. She just raced toward Oliver.

Oliver was too fast for her, though. Holding the net closed with one of his hands, he started scrambling up to his treehouse. The treehouse had a trap-door entrance. As soon as Oliver climbed through it, the door slammed shut. Clara climbed up the ladder, pounding on the door from below.

After a minute, Oliver appeared in the treehouse's single window. He held up a large jar. Inside, Sky Dance fluttered frantically. Addie could see her banging her wings against the glass.

"This is the coolest butterfly I've ever seen!" called Oliver. "And now it's mine!"

He disappeared from the window. Clara gave up and climbed down from the tree, trying to catch her breath. "Okay, so our plan just got a lot more complicated. Let's get out of here and brainstorm."

As Addie led the way back to their

own yard, Shimmer Leaf paused in the air a few times to look back at Oliver's treehouse, her eyes wide with worry. Clara showed them the secret spot she'd found under the deck during their hide-and-seek game. It was barely tall and wide enough for both girls to sit. Addie crawled in after Clara and noticed how soft and cool the dirt felt. *A little gross,* thought Addie, *but also pretty neat.* Shimmer Leaf flitted back and forth between them, up and down in little figure eights. Her wings quivered.

"Whatever we do, we have to do it quickly!" cried the Wishing Wing.

"Can't Sky Dance use her magic to get out of the jar?" asked Clara.

"No," replied Shimmer Leaf, shaking her head. "She needs to be able to fly around something three times to turn it into something else. If the jar's empty, she has nothing to work with."

"Then we should go storm the tree-house!" said Clara.

Addie knew in her heart that wouldn't work. *Storming a treehouse* sounded like something that would get parents involved, and any adult who saw Sky Dance would know she was no ordinary butterfly. No, they couldn't be stormy . . . they had to be *stealthy*.

"We'll sneak in," said Addie.

Clara's angry expression turned thoughtful. "You mean, wait until Oliver's not there?"

"Or lure him out with some kind of distraction," Addie suggested.

Addie was thinking as she was talking.

A picture was forming in her head. What could possibly bring Oliver out of his treehouse after catching the most unusual butterfly he'd ever seen?

Well, that was simple: *Another* unusual butterfly.

Suddenly, the whole plan was clear and complete in Addie's head, like a finished puzzle.

"My sister!" sobbed Shimmer Leaf. "She must be so frightened!"

Addie closed her eyes and listened for Sky Dance's thoughts.

But she heard only silence, and then Shimmer Leaf's shaky voice. "You won't hear her," said the butterfly. "Butterfly magic won't travel through glass."

Addie reached out her palm to the panicked Wishing Wing, and Shimmer Leaf landed on it.

"It's going to be okay," said Addie. "I think I have a plan."

She told Clara and Shimmer Leaf about her idea.

"Blue Rain hates humans, right? Shimmer, you go back to the Grove and tell Blue Rain that a human has captured Sky Dance. Say we need her help because she's tough and strong and speaks her mind. I'll bet she loves being flattered like that. Lead her back to Oliver's yard, and I'll make sure Oliver sees her. While he and I are busy trying to catch Blue Rain, Clara, you sneak into the treehouse and free Sky Dance."

Addie took a deep breath. Her plan sounded just as good out loud as it had in her head.

"That's all possible," said Clara, "except for the part where Oliver will have to set Blue Rain *free* in order to break the enchantment. I don't exactly see him doing that."

"True," agreed Addie. "We'll have to figure that part out later. But at least we have something to start with. Are you guys in?"

"I'm in," Clara said, and high-fived her sister.

Shimmer was silent for a moment, then she zoomed from Addie's palm into the air.

"I'm in too," Shimmer said. The girls still had their hands up, and Shimmer Leaf fluttered against each of them. "We Wishing Wings call that a 'high-fly!'"

Clara giggled, and Addie couldn't help giggling too. She felt a little better now. Maybe everything would work out.

A sudden, loud bark interrupted their laughter.

Addie and Clara crawled out of their hiding spot just in time to see their dog, Pepper, chasing their new kitten, Squish, across the deck and into the yard. The orange kitten bounded up a nearby tree. Then she climbed up even more.

Two days ago, Squish had been a raggedy orange-and-white stuffed animal. Now, thanks to Shimmer Leaf granting Clara's wish for a pet, Squish was a real live kitten that Pepper was, er, having a bit of trouble getting used to.

"Squish!" yelled Clara, running toward the tree, where Pepper was now yipping and running in circles.

Addie quickly followed. When she reached Pepper, she scooped him up in her arms and brought him back to the house. Someone had left the back door slightly open. "Stop making trouble," she scolded the dog as she pushed him inside and slid the door shut.

When Addie turned back to the yard, she saw Clara pulling herself up onto the lowest branch of the tree. Squish was huddled two branches up.

"It's safe now, Squishy!" she called to the blob of orange fur barely visible among the pine needles. "I'll help you get back down!"

Clara grabbed the next branch with one hand and stretched her other arm toward the kitten. But Squish didn't budge. Clara reached higher, her fingertips brushing his side. Addie held her breath. For one second, it looked like Clara was about to grab Squish, and then

the next second, she was sprawled on the ground.

"Ow!' Clara cried.

Addie rushed to her sister. Shimmer Leaf darted toward her too, landing on Clara's chest.

"Are you okay?" asked Addie.

Clara sat up and grabbed her left foot. "My ankle hurts. I think I twisted it when I landed."

Addie turned to Shimmer Leaf, who was still clinging to Clara's shirt. "Can you fix it?"

Shimmer Leaf tapped two of her right legs against the side of her head. "I can definitely help," she said after a few moments of thinking. "But it won't be instant. Do you have something you can wrap around her ankle?"

Addie considered this, then reached

up and touched the ribbon she'd tied around her ponytail that morning. It was Addie's favorite ribbon: pink with black hearts on it. She'd bought it with birthday money at a craft fair. But Clara was hurt.

"Here," said Addie as she pulled the ribbon loose quickly, before she could change her mind. She looped it several times around Clara's ankle, which was already looking swollen, then tied it into a bow.

"Lift her foot as high as you can," said Shimmer Leaf, and Addie did just that.

Shimmer Leaf whooshed into the air and flew the first circle around Clara's ankle, leaving a trail of purple, peach, and mint green behind her as she went. *Maybe I can find a new ribbon, in Shimmer Leaf's colors,* thought Addie as she watched. Shimmer Leaf flew another circle, then a third, until the stripes began flashing and popping like sparklers. When they vanished, Addie saw the result.

Clara's ankle was now wrapped in a thick, soft bandage that was pink with black hearts on it.

"It's got healing magic," said Shimmer Leaf. "But the magic will take a while to work because I'm still a newbie at this stuff. You can't move yet. I'm going to fly on ahead to find Blue Rain. I'll bring her back and meet you in Oliver's yard."

Shimmer Leaf jetted away into the woods. Addie heard a frightened *mew* and both girls looked up at the spot of orange in the tree.

"Poor Squish!" said Clara. "Addie, you need to get him!"

"Me?" asked Addie. "But I've never climbed a tree before. I don't know how!"

"You have to try! It's not that hard."

"How can you say that? You just fell and got hurt!"

Clara gave her a very angry look, then turned away.

She's right, though, thought Addie. *I should at least try.*

If they left Squish in the tree, he might climb higher and higher. They had to get him so they could focus on Sky Dance. She was alone and scared in a glass jar, and they had no idea what Oliver planned to do with her.

Addie stood up, took a deep breath, and jumped for the first branch. But she didn't jump quite high enough, and only brushed it with her outstretched fingertips.

"Hey," said a high, cheerful voice behind her. "It looks like you could use a hand."

Addie turned, and she'd never in her life been so happy to see a bee hovering in front of her face.

"Kirby!" she exclaimed. "We're trying to get our kitten down from that branch, then we've got to help Sky Dance, who's been captured by the boy next door, and there's a New Bloom named Blue Rain and . . . well, it's a long story. We'll fill you in later."

Kirby flew up the tree to get a better look at Squish, then came down to Addie's eye level again. "Normally, I'm not a fan of felines. But they are hopelessly predictable. I know what to do here."

Kirby buzzed straight into Squish's face, bopping the kitten on the nose, then flying just out of reach. Squish stood up.

Kirby landed on the next branch down and started walking in circles.

"Look at me!" he called. "La-de-dah, I'm just a clueless bug. I'd be so easy to catch!"

Without taking his eyes off Kirby, Squish jumped down to the branch.

"Kirby's doing it!" whispered Clara. "He's luring Squish out of the tree!"

Squish reached out his paw to bat at Kirby, but Kirby shot into the air again and flew down to the next branch. They watched the same thing happen. Finally, Kirby flew down to the ground, buzzing and circling and making himself irresistible to a playful kitten.

When Squish came low enough on the tree trunk, Addie grabbed him and put him in Clara's arms.

"You poor thing!" said Clara, rubbing

her face in his fur. Addie could hear his little motorboat purr start up. "Thank you, Kirby!"

Suddenly, Addie heard something else.

Addie, are you there? Addie, please help me!

CHAPTER SIX

*S*ky Dance! Yes, I can hear you!
  Addie stood completely still, as if moving even an inch would break their thought connection.

Shimmer said you wouldn't be able to send messages through the glass, she added.

Addie waited for a reply. The breeze picked up a bit.

It wasn't easy, answered Sky Dance. *I had to calm myself down and use every ounce of magic I've got.*

Stay calm, Addie told her with her thoughts. *We have a plan. We're coming to rescue you AND save Blue Rain.*

Hurry! said Sky Dance. *Oliver said something about showing me to his parents as soon as they came home.*

Suddenly, Clara stood up.

"Hey!" she exclaimed. "My ankle doesn't hurt anymore."

"Awesome!" said Addie. "Do you want me to unwrap it for you?"

"Take off a magical bandage? Are you nuts? I'm keeping this thing on as long as I can."

Addie laughed and shook her head. "Fine. Put Squish in the house and make sure the door is shut tight this time!"

Clara did just that, and when she came back to the tree, her face was glowing with excitement.

"Shimmer Leaf just sent me a message! Our plan is working so far: Blue Rain's on her way to distract Oliver. She loves the idea of teasing him."

"They're expecting me back at the hive," said Kirby, who'd landed on a nearby flower. "I won't go anywhere near that boy. He once tried to catch me to use in a prank!"

"You've already helped a lot," said Clara.

"Thanks again, Kirby," said Addie, then she turned to Clara. "Let's go!" she urged, and they rushed toward Oliver's house.

"What'll we say to him?" Clara asked on the way.

"Follow my lead," Addie replied.

They stepped into Oliver's yard and Addie took a spot directly under the treehouse window.

"Hey, Oliver!" she called.

There was silence for a few moments. Then Oliver's head appeared in the window. He crossed his arms over his chest.

"Oh, it's you. What do you want?"

"We just saw another butterfly come through our yard. This one was even bigger and cooler than the one you caught!"

"Ha!" said Oliver. "I doubt that!"

"Seriously," said Addie. "It was bright blue and purple and *huge!* Did you see it?"

"You're making that up. You're trying to trick me, and it won't work."

Clara stepped up beside Addie. "Fine,

don't believe us. We'll just catch the butterfly first!"

"Go away!" Oliver shouted. He slammed the window of his treehouse shut.

Addie turned to Clara. "What do we do now?"

Clara shrugged. Addie closed her eyes and sent a message to Sky Dance. *Hang in there. We'll figure something out.*

As soon as she thought those words, she heard fluttering behind her. She felt the tip of something graze the top of her hair. Addie looked up . . .

It was Blue Rain!

The Wishing Wing rocketed over their heads, moving faster than Addie'd ever seen one fly. That wasn't normal butterfly flying. That was *angry* flying.

Addie heard another flutter and turned

to see Shimmer Leaf landing on Clara's shoulder.

"Mission accomplished," Shimmer Leaf whispered.

"Clearly," said Addie, watching Blue Rain fly in furious circles around Oliver's backyard.

"Where is he?" shouted Blue Rain. "The human who catches butterflies and puts them in jars?"

Addie pointed at the treehouse and Blue Rain started circling it immediately. *Good thing she doesn't have magic yet,* thought Addie. *Who knows what she'd try to do!*

"Oliver!" Clara yelled up to the closed window. "The butterfly's right here! Come look!"

The window swung open and Oliver's face appeared again, this time with a big scowl on it. But then he spotted Blue Rain jetting past at eye level. His mouth dropped open in amazement. Two seconds later, he was scrambling down the tree, his butterfly net in one hand and another jar in the other.

"I'm going to catch this one first," he teased Addie and Clara. "You two don't even have a net!"

Blue Rain kept flying angrily around the yard. Oliver began chasing her with the net.

"Now's our chance!" whispered Clara. "I'm going to climb up and get Sky Dance!"

"You?" asked Addie.

"Yes, me. You're afraid of heights, remember?"

Addie remembered. It made her cringe, to think about how frightened she'd been.

Clara took a step toward the tree, but Addie found herself reaching out and grabbing her sister's arm.

"Wait. I'll do it. Your ankle may still be healing."

And I'm embarrassed to have this particular fear, she added to herself.

Don't be embarrassed, she heard Sky Dance say. *But it's always good to face your fears. Especially if it means getting me out of this jar!*

Addie smiled to herself, then took a

deep breath. She reached out her arms and grabbed the first branch, putting her foot on the lowest wooden block nailed to the trunk.

Clara ran over to Oliver and pretended to help him. "Look, it's over there!" she called as Blue Rain flew another wide circle around them.

Addie hoisted her body up, first an arm, then a foot. Again, and then again. She was determined not to look down, and determined not to think about how much it would hurt to fall and land on the ground below.

"It went thataway!" Addie heard Oliver shout, and saw him beginning to run toward the treehouse. She had to hurry if she didn't want to be spotted.

One more branch and one more

foothold, and she would be able to open the trapdoor. Addie reached . . . and stepped . . .

She was there! She put her palm on the wooden door and pushed it up. She pulled herself into the treehouse and closed the door just as Oliver was running past the tree.

Addie spotted the jar in a corner of the treehouse. What she saw inside almost broke her heart.

Sky Dance was huddled against the glass, her wings folded around her like a blanket. Her antennae drooped, and her eyes were shut tight.

Addie grabbed the jar and held it up to her face.

"Sky Dance! It's me! I'm here!"

Sky Dance opened her eyes slowly. They lit up as soon as she saw Addie.

Addie wasted no time. She unscrewed the lid and Sky Dance shot out of the jar, leaving a trail of pink and turquoise behind her.

"Oops, sorry," said Sky Dance as she circled back and landed on Addie's shoulder. "I do that when I'm excited."

Addie glanced around the treehouse. There was nothing here except a small rug in the corner with some pillows. Next to it sat a pile of books, a stationery set, and a few empty peanut butter jars, scraped clean. On one wall, Oliver had posted several photographs of himself and a much older boy, smiling for the camera. That must be his big brother.

Oliver was sad, for sure, and the treehouse was a place to be alone with his sadness (and to eat peanut butter, apparently!). It really was like Blue Rain's

enchantment, because the way he acted outside of the treehouse . . . well, that wasn't him.

Despite the fact that Oliver had been nothing but grumpy to Addie so far, she really wanted him to have a wish come true. He really needed one.

"Let's go see if we can help Oliver catch Blue Rain," said Addie as she opened the trapdoor again. Sky Dance flew out, then circled back.

"The coast is clear!" said Sky Dance. "But make it quick!"

It looked even more difficult to climb *down* from a tree than it had been to climb up, but Addie knew this was no time to let fear get the best of her. She went as quickly, and as safely, as she could. Before she knew it, her left foot was touching solid ground.

"Here they come," whispered Sky Dance. "I'm going to make myself scarce."

The butterfly tucked herself into the V between two tree branches just as Oliver, Clara, and Blue Rain rounded the corner from the front of her house.

Blue Rain must have seen Sky Dance, because she came to land on the branch above Sky Dance's hiding place.

"So, you're free now! With my help, of course!"

"Yes," whispered Sky Dance. "Thank you."

"I guess even bossy princesses can be careless. Hopefully you've learned your lesson."

Sky Dance blinked hard a few times, and Addie could tell her friend was trying not to let Blue Rain get to her. Then the butterfly spotted something over

Addie's shoulder and her eyes grew wide. She ducked behind a branch.

"Remember that time you came to visit the Caterpillar Nursery?" continued Blue Rain in her mean voice. "You told me to eat—"

Swish.

The net came down quickly and hard over Blue Rain.

"Got it!" yelped Oliver.

Clara came running up behind him, breathless. When she saw that Oliver had finally caught Blue Rain, she smiled. Then she looked at Addie and silently mouthed the words "Sky Dance?" Addie nodded yes. Clara pumped her fist.

"Set it free, Oliver," said Addie.

"Why should I? Now I have *two* rare butterflies, and everyone's going to want to see them!"

"Oliver, please," urged Clara. "Something wonderful will happen if you just set the butterfly free, I promise."

Oliver frowned. "You can't prank me. I'm the king of pranks."

"We're not pranking," begged Addie. "We swear!"

"No!" he said.

He shook Blue Rain from the net into the jar and slammed the lid on tight.

CHAPTER SEVEN

O liver sat down on the ground and hugged the jar to his chest.

For the first time that day, Addie began to worry that maybe their plan wouldn't work. She took a deep breath. No. She would not give up! Not yet.

"Oliver," she pleaded. "Why do you need to keep this butterfly?"

"Because," said Oliver, his expression turning sad. "I just do."

"That's not a good enough reason!" Clara insisted. "You can't just catch living things and make them yours. Admire them for a few minutes, sure, but not forever."

Oliver was quiet. Addie hoped Clara's words were getting through to him.

Finally, Oliver swallowed hard and said, "I need something to keep me company. I need a . . ." Then Oliver stopped himself, biting his lip. Addie saw the beginnings of tears in his eyes.

"Friend?" she asked softly.

Oliver didn't answer, but he didn't need to. The way he hunched his shoulders and stared at the ground said it all.

"You and Morgan could be friends again," suggested Addie.

"And if you let this butterfly go, we'll be your friends, too," added Clara.

Oliver looked up at them, but then shook his head. "Everybody hates me now. I'm sure you guys do, too."

Blue Rain had finally stopped fluttering inside the jar. Now she was huddled against the glass, her wings drooping. She must have been too tired and dejected to shout insults anymore.

Addie turned to Clara and leaned in close to her sister's ear.

"What do we do now?"

"I don't know," whispered Clara, her voice drained of confidence. "I'm out of ideas."

Addie glanced at the sky to see the sun resting above the treetops. It wouldn't be long before it started setting. They were running short on time.

Whoosh. Whoosh.

It was a strange sound above them. A low-flying bird? Addie looked around, but saw nothing.

Whoosh. Whoosh.

Clara heard it, too. Both girls spun slowly in a circle, trying to locate the source of the noise.

Whoosh. Whoosh. Whoosh. Whoosh.

Louder and faster now! Oliver jumped up; clearly, he'd heard it as well.

"What was that?" he shouted.

"There!" called Clara, pointing excitedly.

Rising out of the woods was the biggest, most brilliant butterfly Addie had ever seen. It was the size of Oliver's treehouse! She was a bit frightened . . . but also amazed . . . and definitely confused. Was this a Wishing Wing?

Oliver's mouth had dropped into a big O. He just whispered, "Whoa," which really did seem like the most appropriate thing to say.

The butterfly drew closer, and suddenly Addie understood.

Clara did, too. "Oh my goodness," she said breathlessly. "It's *all* of them."

This wasn't one enormous butterfly. This was hundreds of Wishing Wings, flying together! In the shape of one giant butterfly! Queen Rose Glow and King Flit Flash were at the top, acting as the butterfly's "head." The wings were a mosaic of every color and pattern Addie could imagine.

Rose Glow must have sensed through her magic that some extra-special help was called for, and all the Wishing Wings had come together to make it happen.

The formation hovered in the air right above Oliver, flapping its wings slowly.

Addie knew what to do next.

"See, Oliver," she said. "This butterfly has a family. She would miss them terribly if you kept her. You know what it's like to miss someone, right?"

Oliver looked at Addie. At first, he seemed embarrassed, but then tears came back to his eyes. He simply bit his lip and nodded.

He reached for the lid of the jar. Addie held her breath and exchanged a hopeful look with Clara. The enormous mass of Wishing Wing butterflies continued to flap its wings.

Oliver lifted the lid.

At first, Blue Rain didn't even seem to notice. She stayed curled up, her eyes closed.

Did that count as setting her free? Addie wondered.

Blue Rain's big, dark eyes popped open now. Her little head snapped up. Her wings straightened out and the colors on them went from dimmed to glowing again.

"Yee-haw!" she squealed, darting straight up into the air. She flew a giant figure eight above them, then circled the giant butterfly formation. The shape fell apart as all the Wishing Wings surrounded Blue Rain. Addie spotted Tiger Streak, with her yellow, orange, and black tiger-stripes, flitting among them. Sky Dance and Shimmer Leaf burst out of their hiding place and flew to join their parents. It was the happiest and most beautiful reunion Addie had ever seen. Eventually, all the Wishing Wings settled onto the branches surrounding the treehouse. It reminded Addie of a Christmas tree covered in colorful ornaments.

"Whoa," Oliver said again, and sank back down to the ground.

Blue Rain paused in mid-air when she heard his voice, then fluttered her way back toward him. She landed on his knee and said, "Hi."

Oliver was quiet. "Double whoa," he finally said.

"I'm Blue Rain. You caught me and set me free, didn't you?"

Oliver nodded, his eyes wide.

"That means I owe you a wish! You have nice eyes, by the way. They're so brown!"

Oliver looked at Addie and Clara. "If this is a prank, it's the best one ever."

"Not a prank," said Clara. "Magic."

"N-n-no such thing," said Oliver,

shaking his head as if he was trying to wake himself up from a dream.

"I hope you'll feel differently after I grant you a wish," said Blue Rain shyly. She sounded so kind and sensitive now that she was no longer under the enchantment. This was the real Blue Rain!

"It's for real," said Addie. "You get just one, so choose carefully." Then she glanced at the sun resting a little lower in the trees. "But choose sort of quickly, too."

"Well, that's easy," Oliver said. "If wishes-come-true were actually a thing, I would wish for my brother to be here. With me. If you can make that happen, then I'll believe in magic butterflies."

Blue Rain tilted her head, deep in thought. She looked over at Sky Dance and Shimmer Leaf, who had landed nearby.

"I'm a wish newbie," Blue Rain said to them, a little embarrassed. "Any suggestions?"

Sky Dance paused, then Addie got a thought message from her.

The photos! In the treehouse!

Addie smiled. "Hang on," she told Oliver and Blue Rain.

She climbed the tree in a matter of seconds. She didn't have to think about where to put each hand and foot, or even to be nervous. It wasn't until she reached the trapdoor that she realized what she'd done. *Hey! Not scared of tree-climbing anymore!*

Addie removed one of Oliver's photos from the treehouse wall and tucked it carefully into her back pocket. She climbed down to the ground again.

"Here," she said, handing the photo to Oliver.

"How'd you know that was in there?" he asked with a frown.

"Never mind that," replied Addie. "Just hold it still."

Oliver gave her a doubtful look, but did as she instructed. Blue Rain took to the air and flew one slow circle around the photo. The trail she left behind was blue, purple, and white, so pretty that Addie wished she could reach out and touch it.

Oliver's jaw dropped as Blue Rain flew her second circle around the photo . . . and then a third.

Her colors started flashing and sparkling, and they all watched as the stripes slowly disappeared.

The photo had disappeared along with them.

"What happened?" asked Oliver, looking around for the photo that was no longer in his hand.

"Wait for it," said Addie. She hoped they wouldn't have to wait too long.

"Oliver!" called a voice. A woman who must be Oliver's mom opened their back door. "Your brother's on the phone!"

Oliver was up and run-ning toward the

house so quickly, it looked like a fast-motion movie. Blue Rain laughed.

"That was fun!" she said. "But wait, why are all the Wishing Wings here, too? And these other humans?"

"You were under an enchantment that tried to keep you from earning your magic," said Sky Dance. "They all helped get you caught and set free before sunset."

"An enchantment!" exclaimed Blue Rain. "Oh, my! I don't even remember coming out of my chrysalis. I hope I didn't say or do anything I might regret."

Addie, Clara, Sky Dance, and Shimmer Leaf all laughed. Maybe someday Blue Rain would hear the whole story, but this wasn't quite the right time.

"Hey, guys!" shouted a voice. Addie turned to see Oliver running out of the house, a phone in his hand. "My brother's coming home for a visit! He'll be here next week!"

"Yay!" called Addie.

"Can we meet him?" asked Clara.

"Of course! When I told him I had two new friends next door, he was so happy!"

Oliver ran back inside with the phone.

Sky Dance turned to Blue Rain. "Nice work. Especially for a beginner!"

"Thanks," said Blue Rain.

"We shall all return to Wishing Wing Grove and celebrate," said Rose Glow, and all the other butterflies chattered enthusiastically.

"We'll see you tomorrow, I bet," said Sky Dance to Addie as the butterflies began to take to the air.

"One more New Bloom to save," said Addie.

"We're pros by now," added Clara. "This one will be a breeze."

Would it?

As Addie watched the sky fill with every fluttering color she'd ever imagined, her heart swelled with wonder and pride. She'd seen and done things in the past few days that she'd never imagined possible. Whatever happened tomorrow, she was ready. She was ready for anything!

TURN THE PAGE FOR A SNEAK PEEK AT ADDIE AND CLARA'S NEXT MAGICAL BUTTERFLY ADVENTURE!

AVAILABLE NOW!

How beautiful!

Red, orange, yellow, green, blue, indigo, and violet. All the colors of the rainbow, in stripes that swirled across Spring Shine's wings.

The brand-new butterfly blinked and looked around, her yellow eyes wide.

Addie held her breath. Would Spring

Shine know she was a Wishing Wing? When Shimmer Leaf had emerged, the dark enchantment had caused her to forget who she was. It had made Tiger Streak think she was a bee. If Spring Shine *did* know who she was, would she still be herself? The enchantment had turned Blue Rain into a cranky, nasty New Bloom who loved to insult everyone. Fortunately, the real Blue Rain was sweet and kind . . . but that had been a *very* unpleasant afternoon.

Spring Shine spotted the other four Wishing Wings, and her eyes grew even wider.

Then she smiled.

"Hello, my friends!" she said in a cheerful voice. She rocketed out of the hollow, and her friends flew in a circle around her, squealing "Welcome!," "You're here!," and "Hooray!"

Addie and Clara watched this happy reunion, and Addie felt a flood of relief. Could it be that the dark enchantment hadn't worked on Spring Shine? Maybe they wouldn't have to fight it anymore.

Spring Shine landed on the tree trunk near the girls, peering at them with curiosity.

Sky Dance landed next to her and said, "Spring Shine, I want you to meet our friends Addie and Clara."

"Humans in Wishing Wing Grove?" chirped Spring Shine. "Wow, I've missed a lot!"

"When the three of us came out," Shimmer Leaf explained, pointing one leg at Tiger Streak and one at Blue Rain, "we were under a dark enchantment designed to keep us from earning our magic. Addie and Clara helped break that enchantment. They're basically the coolest kids ever."

Addie and Clara smiled at each other. Addie thought, *If a magic butterfly thinks I'm cool, maybe it can be true.*

"How do you feel?" Sky Dance asked Spring Shine. "Anything odd? Do all your butterfly parts work?"

Spring Shine fluttered her wings, stretched all six legs, and waved her antennae around in circles. "Everything seems to be in order," she said. "How do my wings look?"

"They're gorgeous!" Addie told her.

"*Super* gorgeous," Clara agreed.

"Really? You're not just saying that, are you? Because when I was a caterpillar, I was the plainest one in the nursery.

Everyone else was a pretty color, but I was just white."

"Come to the Mirror Pool," suggested Sky Dance. "We'll show you."

Sky Dance led the other four butterflies, and Addie and Clara, to a spot behind the Changing Tree. It was a tiny pond ringed with knobby brown vines, the water smooth and clear as glass. Addie peered in and saw her own reflection, then saw Sky Dance land on her shoulder. One vine hung over the pool, stretched between two trees. Spring Shine flitted over to it. She spread her wings wide, took a deep breath, and looked down.

Then she gasped. It was the sound of shock and panic.

"No!" cried Spring Shine, and burst into tears. "Why?" she wailed. "Why?"

Addie and Clara exchanged very

confused looks. Sky Dance flew over to the vine and perched next to Spring Shine.

"What's the matter?" asked Sky Dance. "You don't like your rainbows? I think these wings are absolutely beautiful!"

"Me too!" said Shimmer Leaf. Tiger Streak and Blue Rain added their agreement as well.

"*Rainbows?*" asked Spring Shine. "What rainbows?"

Jennifer Castle is the author of the Butterfly Wishes series and many other books for children and teens, including *Famous Friends* and *Together at Midnight*. She lives in New York's Hudson Valley with her husband, two daughters, and two striped cats, at the edge of a deep wood that is most definitely filled with magic—she just hasn't found it yet.

www.jennifercastle.com

Tracy Bishop is the illustrator of the Butterfly Wishes series. She has loved drawing magical creatures like fairies, unicorns, and dragons since she was little and is thrilled to get to draw magical butterflies. She lives in the San Francisco Bay Area with her husband, son, and a hairy dog named Harry.

www.tracybishop.com